Murder Steampunk Style

by Lisa M. Lane

Grousable Books

This is a short story by Lisa M. Lane.

More information on her other books can be found at https://grousablebooks.com.

This is a work of fiction. Historical figures have been reimagined by the author based on information about their lives, but there is no intention to laud or disparage them in any way. Any resemblance of other characters to any actual person, living or dead, is purely coincidental.

Published by Grousable Books
Encinitas, California
ISBN 979-8-9869845-6-8

"The key to steampunk," said the sonorous voice of Vernon Sledge, "is that it contains within it the essence of the British Victorian experience. The efforts of outsiders to bring neo-Victorianism to life have been in vain precisely because the Victorian way of life is not patterned into their heritage. In England it is still alive."

The forty or so attendees listened with rapt attention, nodding their heads. The panel was the first at the 19th Annual Steampunk Convention. All the event rooms at the San Diego City and Village Hotel had been reserved for the occasion, with the assumption that the literary panels would be the best-attended. For what was steampunk without the stories, the novels, the characters?

High school English teacher Mrs. Emily Carter was quite sure she didn't know. But that was why her students had wanted her to come. Ever since it had emerged in class that Mrs. Carter didn't know steampunk novels from pulp fiction, Jason, Keisha, and Jeremy had pleaded with her to attend, even buying her a ticket. She agreed when they promised to serve as her interpreters.

"Are you saying, Mr. Sledge," asked the panel chairman, "that steampunk novels must be created by British authors?"

"No, of course not. I'm saying steampunk must be created by English authors. Preferably men."

A grumble rolled through the room. People turned to each other, asking if Sledge could possibly mean what he said. English only? Men only? Annie Lee had written a best-selling steampunk novel only last year!

"Well," the chairman said, amused, "I would say that is a good place to conclude our panel. May we have a round of applause for our guests: Roland Chubb, Joyce Hall, and Vernon Sledge?"

There was enthusiastic applause.

"And now our guests would be willing to take some questions. Please come to the microphones in the side aisles."

Only a few people moved to the microphone, but one of them was Keisha. She was in costume, as most of the attendees were, her hair ironed and pulled back into a sleek bun under a dark blue hat featuring an array of plastic fruit. The petticoat of her gown could be heard rustling as she moved.

"Mr. Sledge," she said, her voice firm, "you must know that we have many successful female writers of steampunk, and that some are American. Some"—she looked pointedly at Joyce Hall, author of *The Mission Bay Fliers*—"are even from here in San Diego. Are you trying to take us back to the 1860s in life as well as literature?"

There was a smattering of applause.

"Well, miss," Sledge said in a voice dripping with condescension, "when you are a bit older, perhaps you will see the connection between the mores of the Victorian age, which should be preserved, and the technological achievements, originally English, that continue to this day. All of which," he added, "were created by men."

"They were created by men," said Keisha, "because men didn't allow women the time or the freedom to create them."

"That may be true. But they were invented by men, all the same."

Keisha returned to her seat, her face burning. The other questions were few, and primarily regarded the plot devices used in Sledge's current best-seller, *The*

Chrononautic Air Machine Wars. Jason tugged Mrs. Carter's sleeve, and the four rose and left for the courtyard.

"Lemonade or punch?" offered a young woman in a parlor-maid outfit, standing behind a table. The breeze blew in the palms above the courtyard, but it was still quite warm. "Lemonade, please," said Jeremy, collecting drinks for the group. Jason was looking at his conference booklet.

"All right," he said, as they took a seat on one of the green benches in the shade. "There's another author panel later, and a costume workshop. But right now, it's the workshop on swords and umbrellas."

"Why swords and umbrellas?" asked Mrs. Carter. It seemed an odd combination.

"Self-defense," said Keisha. "I'm in."

"Me, too," said Jeremy. He was on the school fencing team.

Jason and Mrs. Carter shrugged. "Maybe Mrs. C. and I can go look at the vendors in the Market Hall," suggested Jason.

Keisha and Jeremy left, and Jason and Mrs. Carter sipped their lemonade. A dressed-up couple was coming down the courtyard. The man had full dark whiskers, a top hat with goggles perched above the brim, a green brocade waistcoat, and a large copper contraption with tubes covering one arm.

"He looks for all the world like a cross between Charles Dickens and the Borg," said Mrs. Carter to Jason under her breath.

He smiled. "What's a Borg?"

The woman accompanying this gentleman wore a leather corset covered with gears and clock faces, and a long black-and-white striped skirt. Mrs. Carter at first thought her silver-topped cane was an affectation, but as she limped along it became obvious she needed it. The couple took a seat on the opposite bench.

"New to the conference?" asked the gentleman with a smile. They were fairly obvious since their costumes weren't expensive. Jason was wearing an explorer's outfit with khaki pants and a brown leather jacket. His pith helmet had a fan fixed in the front; he'd gotten it at Disneyland. Mrs. Carter was dressed in a pale blue Edwardian day dress she'd rented from the costume place near the airport. She hadn't gotten accessories, though, and knew her earrings didn't match the look.

"Yes. My friends and I brought our English teacher," said Jason. Mrs. Carter wondered at him being so forthcoming, until it occurred to her that he didn't want anyone thinking she was his mother. Or, God forbid, grandmother.

"And you look charming, English teacher, if I may say so," the man said, tipping his hat. "I am Milo Pennyfeather and this is my amanuensis, Honoria."

"Your costumes are beautiful," said Mrs. Carter. "Do you come here every year?"

"Oh, yes, since we were teens," said Honoria. "Our whole apartment is decorated in steampunk style." She leaned forward and spoke more quietly. "I'm an accountant in the modern world. He works at the DMV."

"My dear, it isn't polite to share intimate details on first acquaintance," Milo said with a wink. "Have you two been to the Market Hall? They have some wonderful accessories this year."

"Then let's go look," said Mrs. Carter, rising. "It was very nice to meet you, and I'm sure we'll see you again."

"What's an amanuensis?" Jason asked once they were out of hearing.

"An assistant, scribe, and inspiration, typically."

"Like a muse?"

"Even more serviceable than a muse. An amanuensis is of practical help."

The Market Hall room was large. The walls had been decorated so that it looked like a bazaar. There were scarves tacked up, in paisley and diamond patterns, and a large clock in the center shaped like the Eiffel Tower, its pendulum tocking away loudly.

At one table, an array of steampunk jewelry was laid out: clockwork ear cuffs, leather wrist gauntlets, connected silver rings that covered all four fingers. Some featured mother-of-pearl or tiny devices like pistons or bicycle wheels.

As Jason was looking at a leather wristband with an embedded compass, the vendor, a large woman dressed as an African explorer, gushed a hello to a new customer. The woman approaching the table was in a tall wooden wheelchair. Her full gray hair was swept up in a fashionable style, and she wore a small hat with black lace covering her forehead. Her gown fitted her trim form perfectly and was solid black with sparkles of tiny jet, the silver points on her black leather gloves the only relief from the black.

"Mrs. Jewel! I heard you were here. Is there something I can help you with?"

"Black lace gloves, please," she replied in a smooth voice.

"Finger-free, of course?"

"Of course."

The vendor produced the pair and took Mrs.

Jewel's credit card. Jason realized he was staring when she looked up at him, smiled, and nodded.

"Good day, young man."

Jason tipped his hat as she slipped the gloves into her purse, then backed her wheels and turned away toward the other booths. He spoke quietly to the vendor.

"Was that Mrs. Alexandria Jewel?" he asked, a bit of awe in his voice.

"Yes, indeed. Author of the Glasswork Mechanism series."

"And the one who sued another author for stealing her work."

"Oh, yes, but that was a long time ago. Do you like the wristbands?"

Mrs. Carter appeared, holding up two earrings that looked like calipers with balls on the end.

"How do these look? The man at that table told me they were steam engine governors."

"They look fabulous, Mrs. C."

They found Keisha waiting for them at the end of the aisle. In the far corner was a large object that looked like a vehicle. Jason recognized it right away.

"That's H. G. Wells' time machine!" he said. He had read the book only the month before.

Mrs. Carter had only seen the movie. This machine, while resembling the one in the film, was fancier, with complex gears and an exterior like rubbed brass.

"They say it's real," Keisha said.

"Who says?" asked Jason.

"I do, for one," said a voice behind them. They turned to see a tall man dressed as Sherlock Holmes, holding a meerschaum pipe in one slim hand and wearing a houndstooth cape. He tipped his deerstalker to Keira and Mrs. Carter, observing them with intelligent eyes.

"Sherlock Holmes, at your service. I arrived here in that most venerable machine, from London, the year 1894."

"Goodness," said Mrs. Carter, not knowing what else to say.

"Then you must have just solved the Final Problem," said Jeremy with a grin, "and been killed in the battle with Moriarty."

Holmes nodded sagely. "Indeed, the world thinks me dead. But I am not. I am here, as you can see. If you'll excuse me, I believe I'll withdraw to smoke my pipe outside. I hear that smoking is not welcome in here." He made his way through the crowd.

"Wonderful costume," said Mrs. Carter. "And that

voice. Such confidence. I almost believed he was Holmes himself."

Jason and Keisha laughed.

"Knows his stuff," said Jason. "Do you think he brought Watson with him?"

The Mad Hatter Tea Party was set for 2 p.m. The ballroom had been turned into a tearoom, with long tables covered in white cloths featuring centerpieces of teapots, each with a stuffed dormouse peeking out the top. A woman in a March Hare costume greeted everyone at the door and took their tickets.

At first, the tea party was quite organized. Everyone sat at the place setting designated with their name card. Mrs. Carter and her students were seated together at one end of a long table. She saw a table where an uncostumed group was sitting, including Vernon Sledge, and assumed that was the writers' table. Milo and his amanuensis were seated at the other end of their table, and they waved a cheery hello. The room was filled with female adventurers, airship pilots, engineers, and mad scientists. A shiny brass automaton was seated at the head table, but he didn't move. They saw Sherlock Holmes standing against the wall, observing rather than joining in.

"That's weird," said Keisha, pointing to a man at the far table near the dais, also dressed as Holmes.

"Two Sherlock Holmes!" said Jeremy, laughing. "Didn't anyone want to play Dr. Watson?"

"Watson's second fiddle," said Jason. "Everyone would want to be Holmes."

A crew of volunteers, dressed in red livery, presented multi-tiered plates of tea sandwiches and cakes to each group, then went around pouring tea.

A large man with a huge hat, decorated with a sign saying, "In this style 10/6," rose at the front of the room to address the partiers.

"Good afternoon, everyone! I hope you are enjoying your tea. Now, I have one question: how is a raven like a writing desk?"

There was laughter around the room, followed by a flurry of activity on the part of the liveried servers. They were busily going around the tables and moving all the place cards to other locations. Mrs. Carter's place card was whisked away and taken to the next table at the end. People were rising, grabbing their teacups and cake, and moving to where their place card had been taken.

Within a few minutes, the room was pandemonium, with everyone following their place cards and laughing, sitting in their new spot for a few minutes and greeting everyone there, having a sip or two of tea, and moving on. The rustle of petticoats, clattering of cogs and metal parts, people excusing themselves and laughing, continued for over twenty minutes. Finally, the Hatter rose again, tapping his teapot with an oversized spoon to get attention.

"We hope you've enjoyed our tea party! Now everyone, get out!"

Mrs. Carter had no idea where her entourage had ended up, so she simply did what the others were doing and moved slowly and breathlessly to the door, assuming she'd find them in the courtyard.

Behind her there was a scream, and it wasn't a scream of laughter. One of the liveried servers was having hysterics, and it was obvious why. People turned and froze as they saw the figure of Vernon Sledge collapsed over his place setting, not moving.

A group quickly formed around what proved to be a dead Vernon Sledge. This was verified by a mad scientist, who said he was an emergency room nurse in real life. The conference organizer, Nero Fortnum, a short, mustachioed man in a red waistcoat and pin-striped trousers, had been summoned by one of the volunteers. He spoke with the nurse. The security guard for the convention arrived and asked everyone to step back from the body and clear the room. He covered Mr. Sledge with a tablecloth, then asked Mr. Fortnum to seal off the area.

By this point, Mrs. Carter had been found by her students. The crowd was now outside the ballroom door, which remained open. She saw the security guard take out his phone and dial 911 for the police.

"They won't be able to come," said Jason at her shoulder.

"Why not?"

"There's a Sig-alert on the I-8. Semi overturned and is blocking both directions. Jammed up all the way west to Sea World and east to La Mesa."

The security guard came over to close the door, but he caught sight of Mrs. Carter.

"Well!" he said, with a smile. "It's Mrs. Carter, isn't it?"

He looked familiar, but it took a few seconds before she could place him. It was Jesús Morales, one of the students in her very first class at Hillcrest High.

"Jesús! How nice to see you. It's been years!"

"You look amazing," he said. Then he saw the students and remembered himself. "I'm afraid I have to close this door." He looked around and motioned her inside. "Excuse me, kids—I just need Mrs. Carter for a moment."

Mrs. Carter stood just inside the ballroom as he closed the door.

"Mrs. Carter, I remember your class," said Jesús. "I loved reading the mystery stories especially. You said you were always able to know who done it."

She smiled. It was true; it was hard to fool her in a mystery story.

"I usually do," she said modestly. She saw over his shoulder that vendor screens were being placed around the table where poor Vernon Sledge was slumped.

"Well, thing is, I just called the police, and they can't get here. Coroner neither. Big crash on the 8."

"I heard."

"I don't suppose you could give us a hand?"

Mrs. Carter had seen only one dead body, and that was of her grandmother, who had died in the hospital.

But this was all so intriguing.

"Yes, of course."

He led her over to the body, then held up the tablecloth so she could see. She could only look for a second.

"Poison, clearly."

"Yes." She swallowed.

Jesús put the sheet back apologetically. "I'm sorry. Death is rarely clean or pretty. I should know."

She looked at him.

"Afghanistan," he said.

Mrs. Carter was still trying to keep her tea and cake down as Jesús escorted her back toward the door.

"I guess I have to question everyone." He looked dismayed. "We hired six guards from Advanced Secure Co, but I stationed them around the area to prevent people leaving."

The man dressed as Sherlock Holmes was waiting inside the door.

"I'm sorry, sir, but you'll need to leave the area," said Jesús, surprised.

"I believe I can be of assistance. My card." He presented Jesús with an embossed ivory card that said, "Sherlock Holmes. Private Investigator."

Mrs. Carter looked up at him. His face was calm

and assured, not at all like a crackpot.

"Sir, I've asked everyone to leave this room—" Jesús began, but Holmes was already moving toward the body.

"I do not believe it necessary to question everyone." He looked back toward the door, his eyes focused above it. "I believe you have operating a version of the kinesigraph?"

"A what?" Jesús and Mrs. Carter looked above the door and saw a dark half-globe of glass.

"A chrono-photographic gun, as the French say."

Jesús shook his head.

"I apologize," said Holmes. "We are in America. You would say kinetograph?"

"It's a security camera."

"Precisely. I was standing there"—he pointed to the side wall—"during the entire tea party. I heard its gears turn and noticed a blue illumination. Where is the paper or film of the event?"

Jesús blinked several times.

"Is there footage from the party?" asked Mrs. Carter gently.

"Yes, there would be."

"Then perhaps it could be developed in good time," said Holmes. He was speaking very simply, as if to a child. "Then we could analyze it."

Mrs. Carter stared at the man. Surely he must be an actor. He had the part down pat.

"First, I must make an announcement to the attendees," said Jesús stiffly. "If you'll excuse me?"

Now even Jesús was talking like it was the Victorian age. Mrs. Carter stifled a smile as he opened the door.

Her students were waiting, trying not to look eager for information.

Jesús looked out at the crowd in the courtyard. There must have been sixty people standing around. He spoke to Mrs. Carter's students.

"I need to get information from people."

"We can help," said Jason, raising his hand like in class. Keisha and Jeremy raised theirs too. "You want to know where everyone was and what they saw, right?"

"Yes, that would be great." He looked around. "Do you need notebooks or paper?"

The trio held up their phones. "We're on it," said Jason.

Jesús jumped up onto the edge of a palm planter so the attendees could see him.

"Everyone! Everyone! The police are unable to be here yet, so I've deputized these young people to get information from you. If you actually witnessed Mr. Sledge expire, please see me immediately. If not, please talk to one of the deputies."

Milo raised his hand. "Mr. Guard? It's almost time for the historians' panel, and then the model airship exhibition. May we proceed with those?"

Jesús said, "After you've spoken to a deputy, yes." He turned to Nero Fortnum. "I take it this room will no longer be needed?"

"No." Although Fortnum had organized the entire conference, which had been no mean feat, he looked rather dazed as Jesús took command.

"Then the conference may continue. But no one may leave the area. I have security guards stationed at the event gates and in the kitchens."

Jesús turned back to Mrs. Carter. "The tea party seemed pretty noisy."

"It was the Mad Hatter's Tea Party. They kept moving place settings around, and people followed their place setting, bringing their cake and tea with them. It was crazy for about twenty minutes." She looked around. "Where is Sherlock Holmes?"

"Uh oh. We must have left him inside."

They went back in to find Holmes looking at the body under the tablecloth.

"Whoever you are, I need you to leave this room and join the others." Jesús was getting irritated.

"As I thought," said Holmes. "Poison. Likely cyanide. There wasn't time for anything else. He was alive and well when the party began."

"Or he had a heart attack." Jesús frowned.

"Unlikely. I think you'll find that no one noticed anything amiss. But I did notice one thing."

"What is that?"

"I'd like to look at the film first."

Jesús looked over at Mrs. Carter, who shrugged. Whoever this man was, he seemed to think he was a detective. Another pair of eyes, under the circumstances, might come in handy.

"This confirms my suspicions," said Holmes, as they looked at the film on the old monitor in the kitchen. "There simply wasn't time. His head is down and he isn't moving by the time of the third seat change."

"What does that mean?" said Jesús, frowning.

"It means he must have been poisoned before the amusement began."

"Then it must have been someone at the writer's table," said Mrs. Carter.

"Precisely, madam. Who was at that table?"

Nero Fortnum took a piece of paper out of his coat pocket as they all returned to the ballroom.

"I have the list here with the seating chart. Mr. Sledge, of course. Then Annie Lee, Roland Chubb, Joyce Hall, Alexandria Jewel, and Boz."

Holmes appeared not to be listening. He had removed the tablecloth from the body and was lifting a teacup to his nose.

"Not cyanide," he said decisively.

"How do you know?" asked Jesús.

"There is a fair percentage of people who cannot detect the bitter almond scent of cyanide. Fortunately, I can."

He began circling the table, smelling all the cups. Then he began on the plates.

"This is nuts," mumbled Jesús.

The ballroom door opened, and the other man dressed as Sherlock Holmes peeked his head in, then saw them and entered. He addressed himself to Jesús.

"I am Sherlock Holmes, at your service." He seemed not to notice the taller Sherlock Holmes standing next to him. "I am the finest detective in the world."

"I am Jesús, and you must leave immediately." His voice sounded tentative rather than forceful. He hadn't been able to get the other Holmes to leave, after all.

The taller Holmes looked down his nose at the newcomer, then his face lit up.

"Ah, a doctor! Excellent."

The shorter man looked shaken.

"What do you mean, a doctor? I am Sherlock Holmes." He tipped his deerstalker for effect.

"You're a doctor, as can easily be seen by the indentation around your collar, where your stethoscope usually presses."

"That's ridiculous," the man said, fingering his collar.

"Your hands are raw," continued Holmes, raising the man's hand from his side, "not only from repeated washing, but perhaps from the use of carbolic spray during surgery?"

The man looked uneasily at the assembled company.

"I—I—I have a latex allergy."

"I see a rectangular impression in your trouser pocket that is no doubt a small communication device, which I believe hospitals continue to use despite the newer telephonic portables. And no one can mistake that smell of the infirmary."

The new Holmes looked beaten.

"I would appreciate your help with the body," said Holmes in a kinder tone. "I am quite sure he was poisoned, but I do not believe he ingested it."

The doctor began examining the body at the top of the head, and slowly worked his way downward, moving clothing as needed. Holmes turned to Jesús, Fortnum, and Mrs. Carter.

"Now, what we need is a motive. Do we know who might have despised the victim?"

"None of these authors particularly liked each other," said Fortnum. "They each wrote very different types of books, but the steampunk audience is not large."

The door opened again, and Keisha, Jason, and Jeremy entered, cell phones in hand. They looked curiously at Holmes but spoke to Jesús.

"We've talked to everyone, but nobody saw anything except the last group coming back to the table," said Jason. "They just saw Vernon Sledge slumped over."

"So," said Keisha, "we tried to find out who might have hated him."

"Focusing on the people at the writers' table,"

added Jeremy.

"What did you find out?" asked Mrs. Carter.

Keisha looked at her phone. "Annie Lee and Roland Chubb are friends. They have the same publisher. Mr. Chubb doesn't like Joyce Hall because he says she really writes romances and just calls them steampunk."

"Boz and Roland Chubb aren't speaking to each other because their book covers look too much alike," said Jason.

"Alexandria Jewel said that Boz was jealous of Vernon Sledge because he was interviewed by three different TV programs the same week," said Jeremy.

"Excuse me?" The doctor was beckoning to Holmes, and the others trailed behind him. He held up Sledge's dead hand. "There is every sign that he was poisoned. I think the entry point may have been these wounds."

They peered and could just see four little holes, each near a knuckle on the left hand.

"I see," said Holmes. "A toxin, then?"

The doctor nodded. "And you're looking for something very fast acting?"

"Indeed."

"The only thing I've seen like this was a case from South America during the 1980s. The patient was in

Surinam."

"The Dutch colony?" inquired Holmes.

The doctor blinked. "It was some kind of blue frog. The coating on its skin would kill a man in minutes."

"Thank you, Doctor." Holmes turned to the three students. "And thank you for the information you collected. And now, I am interested in what people were wearing."

Annie Lee, Roland Chubb, Joyce Hall, Alexandria Jewel, and the author known as Boz were seated at the table near the door and rose as Jesús approached.

"Why have we been ordered in here?" Joyce Hall said, bristling. "I was enjoying the talk on A Gentleman's Guide to the Martian Language."

"I was speaking to a group of young actors about adapting my short stories," said Roland Chubb. The others began to chime in with their own activities.

"Enough!" said Holmes. The authors took notice of him for the first time.

"Who is this?" asked Alexandria Jewel, her tone dripping disdain.

"This man is assisting in our investigation," said Jesús, trying not to look sheepish.

"Oh, for Chrissake," said Boz. "Surely the police are on their way by now? This man is nothing other than a fan dressed for cosplay!"

"Boz, is it?" asked Holmes. "After the Charles Dickens pseudonym, I assume. Would you turn so I may see your full costume?"

"It's not a costume. It's my business suit," grumbled Boz, but turned.

"Everyone, please?" demanded Holmes. They all turned.

"And all of you were wearing to the tea party exactly what you are wearing and carrying now?" They all nodded.

"Now may I see inside your bags, please?" There was grumbling, but they opened their bags. Keisha and Jeremy used the flashlight app on their phones and peered inside.

When they were done, Holmes retreated with the group a few paces away from the writers.

"Did any of you see anything that could cause small wounds?" he asked quietly. They shook their heads.

"Mr.—um—Holmes," said Jason. "They aren't all wearing exactly what they were wearing at the tea party. I saw Alexandria Jewel buy the lace gloves she's wearing now. She was wearing leather gloves at the tea party."

Holmes smiled. "Ah! Please examine the rubbish boxes around this room and just outside the door."

The students made a face.

"Just on the top." He turned to Jesús. "When the police arrive, ask them to arrest Miss Alexandria Jewel. The murder weapon should present itself shortly."

When the police arrived, they took into their possession a pair of leather gloves with small daggers on the fingers, and arrested Alexandria Jewel. But it had been difficult to explain everything completely without Sherlock Holmes. Mrs. Carter, her students, and Mr. Fortnum went in search of him.

"I found the dagger gloves in the trash can near the kitchen," said Keisha. "How did Holmes know?"

Jason frowned. "Alexandria Jewel must have arranged to be seated next to Mr. Sledge. She planned to poison the tips of the little daggers on her gloves, then touch his hand at some point. But this morning she realized her hands would be bare after the murder, since she'd need to get rid of the gloves. So she bought the lace ones for afterwards."

"But why kill Vernon Sledge?" asked Jeremy.

"I wonder," said Mrs. Carter. "Years ago there was a copyright case against Vernon Sledge. He was accused of passing off another author's work as his own."

"*The Crystal Buccaneer*," agreed Nero Fortnum. "It was a huge best-seller. Appeared on every top fiction list. People read it who had never read a steampunk story in their lives. Miss Jewel said she wrote it. I'd completely forgotten, it was so long ago."

"You mean Vernon Sledge stole a book from a female writer?" Keisha's eyes were wide.

"We must tell Mr. Holmes," said Jason. They searched the last few rooms and the courtyard, but no one had seen him. They walked the aisles of the Market Hall. As they were passing the time machine, Jason paused and walked over to it, placing his hand on the shining brass. The others stopped.

"What is it?" asked Mrs. Carter.

Jason smiled, knowing that Mr. Holmes would not be talking to the police. "It's still warm."